Secret of the Black Widow

11/25/02

By
Eugene M. Gagliano

Danielle,
    I hope you enjoy my first
published children's book.
    Remember that family & good
friends are life's most precious
gifts.
    May you be blessed this holiday
season.

WM KIDS   WHITE MANE KIDS
SHIPPENSBURG, PENNSYLVANIA

Merry Christmas,
Mr. G.

This White Mane Books publication
was printed by
Beidel Printing House, Inc.
63 West Burd Street
Shippensburg, PA 17257-0708 USA

The acid-free paper used in this book meets the guidelines for permanence and durability of the Committee on Production Guidelines for Book Longevity of the Council on Library Resources.

For a complete list of available publications
please write
White Mane Books
Division of White Mane Publishing Company, Inc.
P.O. Box 708
Shippensburg, PA 17257-0708 USA

Library of Congress Cataloging-in-Publication Data

Gagliano, Eugene M.
    Secret of the black widow / by Eugene M. Gagliano.
        p. cm.
    Summary: In the spring of 1890 in the Wyoming Territory, twelve-year-old Chad faces his fears and becomes friends with the reclusive Foster family.
    ISBN 1-57249-286-4 (alk. paper)
    [1. Frontier and pioneer life--Wyoming--Fiction. 2. Wyoming--Fiction.] I. Title.

PZ7.G124 Se 2001
[Fic]--dc21

                                                                    2001056753

To my wife, Carol,
for her love, support, and belief in me

Contents

Acknowledgments

With special thanks to Sandy Jelly and George Schafer for their special help in making this book possible.

Chapter 1

Red Fox

The scream from the direction of the widow Foster's cabin made the hair rise on the back of Chad's neck.

"Scared?" James Junior asked.

"No, I just don't think it's right. She ain't never bothered me none," Chad said, but in his heart he knew the truth. He was afraid.

"My dad says she's evil," Brett added.

"Afraid she might do somethin' to you, Chad?" Junior teased.

"I told you, I just don't think it's right." Chad looked at his dusty boots. "Come on, we're goin' to be late for school."

The late April sunshine shone over the prairie, lighting the widow Foster's shabby pioneer cabin, as Chad and the other two boys approached the curve in the rutted wagon trail. A faint plume of ashen gray smoke rose from the stone chimney.

"Maybe she's waitin' for Chad to stop by," James said. "Maybe—"

"Look," Brett interrupted. "There's the Black Widow now."

Chad felt uneasy. He pushed his straw hat down tight on his head. The widow appeared in front of the log cabin, which stood about 50 yards from the trail. She wore a black dress and a slight breeze tugged at her bonnet, as she glided toward the well. Chad figured she didn't see him or the other boys, or she pretended not to.

"Can you see her?" Junior asked.

"No. She's too far away," Brett answered.

Chad watched the widow lower her bucket into the well. He shifted his gaze toward the cabin. A little boy stood staring in the doorway. His bleached white hair glowed in the sunlight. He looked like a straw doll. A girl stepped out of the doorway and kissed the boy's cheek. Chad knew her name was Aubrey Foster and she was 11, one year younger than himself. He watched as Aubrey grabbed a worn woolen shawl from a hook by the door.

"Bye, Mama," Aubrey said shaking her fiery-red braids. Her mother mumbled something without looking up.

"Here comes the Red Fox," Junior chuckled. "Maybe Chad could ask her what her mother's hidin'."

Like everyone else, Chad wondered why the widow always wore a black veil when she went to town? Why she always turned away from people and spoke softly like a light breeze? Nobody knew much about her. Why did it seem so important to see her face up close without the veil? Chad knew it was none of his business.

Aubrey walked up the trail a little before Junior and Brett ran up behind her.

Chad deliberately stayed back a ways.

"Hey, Red Fox," Junior said. "Got any new freckles?"

Aubrey kept walking. She clenched her fist and ignored Junior.

Junior reached up behind her and pulled at her braid.

"Ouch!" Aubrey turned and glared at Junior. "Leave me alone or I'll—"

"Or you'll what?"

Aubrey stomped her foot. Her face tightened. She turned and hurried up the trail toward the Chokecherry Creek schoolhouse. Junior and Brett walked faster to catch up with her.

Chad wished there were other boys his age to be friends with besides Junior and Brett.

"Leave her alone." Chad kicked at a stone in the trail.

"What did you say?" Junior gave Chad a mean look.

"Leave her alone—so we can go to the creek. I saw some big fish in the bend yesterday."

"I suppose," Junior said.

Chad took off at full speed. "Last one to the creek is a rotten egg." Junior stood tall for a 12 year old, but Chad ran faster.

The water in the bend flowed smooth and deep. Chad and the other boys slapped ripples into the icy water with their hands. Shadowy fish darted beneath the water. A cool breeze rustled the tattered grasses left from last summer. Chad breathed the earthy smell of spring. He heard the clang of the school bell and sighed. He wished he could watch the creek all morning.

When Chad reached the log schoolhouse, his teacher, Miss Maple Bryant, greeted the boys with a stern look.

"You three were almost late again. Got a touch of spring fever?" Her pinched lips melted into a smile. "Come on in. We have work to do."

"Yes, ma'am." Chad hurried in. Chad liked Miss Bryant and he thought she liked him too. Miss Bryant made the children work hard, but she was fair. Chad liked her reddish brown hair which she tied neatly in a bun. Miss Bryant wore calico, high-collared dresses and she smelled sweet and clean. Chad thought she looked like a prairie meadow in bloom.

The chilly morning air left the one-room schoolhouse as the heat from the small, black wood stove reached out into the room. The rough wooden bench made sitting difficult, as Chad stared blankly at his slate board. A meadowlark's sweet song pulled his attention toward the window. He could see down the trail and his thoughts turned to the widow. He wondered whether she really was evil. If she was, then he surely had good reason to be afraid of her.

Chapter 2
Scared

Aubrey seemed nice for a girl. She never talked much at school. The other children teased her because of her red hair and freckles; besides, her mother was the Black Widow. She spent a lot of time by the creek at recess. Nothing wrong with that, Chad thought. He liked to do that too. Aubrey always knew the answers to Miss Bryant's questions. Chad guessed Aubrey liked school, but she didn't have any friends.

Chad could't keep his mind on school. He stared out the window and worried. What if Junior kept after him about sneaking up on the Black Widow? What would he do?

"Did you hear what I said?" Miss Bryant asked.

"What?" Chad looked toward the front of the room.

"Did you hear the question?"

"No, ma'am."

"You do have spring fever!" Miss Bryant said.

The rest of the morning passed slowly. Chad couldn't stop thinking about the widow. Chad ate lunch under an old cottonwood tree with Junior and Brett. The buds on the cottonwood tree swelled, ready to burst into green. Chad took out his sandwich of cornbread and molasses. His stomach grumbled like distant thunder.

"Mama says our cat's gonna have kittens soon," Chad said. "Her belly's stretched way out and you can feel the little critters kickin' when you put your hand on it."

"You gonna drown them?" Junior asked.

"What for?"

"My pa says the only good cat is a dead cat."

"Shucks, no. My mama says cats eat mice."

"Well, if I was you, I'd drown them."

Chad changed the subject. He couldn't change Junior's mind about cats.

"Brett, your pa fixin' to buy you a horse like he promised?" Chad asked wiping some molasses from his chin.

"I reckon someday. Seems like there's always somethin' that needs to be done first."

"Hey look," Junior said. "The Red Fox is pickin' posies. Ain't that sweet?"

Chad followed Junior and Brett over to where Aubrey knelt picking some tiny yellow flowers. Why couldn't Junior leave her alone?

"Need any help?" Junior teased.

"No, thank you."

"Say, me and the boys were wonderin' about your ma. Weren't we, boys?"

Brett nodded in agreement. Chad looked away.

"How come your mama always wears that black veil into town?"

"Ever see your mama's face, Aubrey?" Brett laughed.

Aubrey looked the other way and picked some more flowers.

"What about those strange sounds that come from behind your cabin? What are they?" Junior knocked the flowers out of her hand. "Sounds like your mama's boiling your little brother in oil. What's wrong with your brother? Has he got some kind of spell on him?"

"You leave my brother out of this! You leave us alone," Aubrey shouted. She clenched her fists. "I hate you, James Junior!" Aubrey ran back to the safety of the schoolhouse. Her braids snapped back and forth behind her.

"I was just wonderin'," Junior said.

Brett laughed.

"Chad, you're awful quiet. Don't you wonder about that Foster family? You afraid?" Junior taunted.

"I ain't afraid!"

"You are too."

"Am not."

"Well if you ain't afraid, then I dare you to run up to the widow Foster and look her square in the eye."

"I can't!" Chad exclaimed. "I told you before. It ain't right. It ain't none of our business."

"You're chicken," Junior snickered.

"I ain't chicken. I'll show you after school," Chad blurted out. The words had hardly left his lips when he realized what he'd said. He couldn't back out now. He'd made a mistake and he knew it. He was scared.

Chapter 3

Straight in the Eye

By the time Miss Bryant dismissed school, Chad felt sick to his stomach. What if he got caught trying to sneak up on the Black Widow? No telling what she might do. If his parents found out, he'd be in big trouble.

"You ready?" Junior grinned.

"Sure," Chad tried not to sound nervous. "Let's go."

Chad, Junior, and Brett hurried down the trail toward the run-down Foster place. Chad wanted to get there before Aubrey got home.

After the long winter, the warm breeze felt good on Chad's face. Overhead a winged formation of geese aimed itself northward. The loud honking caught Chad's attention.

"Geese!" Chad pointed toward the cloudy sky.

"There must be hundreds," Brett added.

"Sure are noisy critters," Junior complained. "Come on. We ain't got time to stand around lookin' at some dumb birds."

"Geese are smarter than your pet chickens," Brett dared to say.

"Shut up," Junior said.

Brett nudged Chad. "Wonder what happened to the widow's husband? Suppose she got rid of him—you know what I mean?"

"Reckon anythin's possible," Chad answered.

"Suppose she's wanted some place by the sheriff?" Brett whispered.

"You fool," Junior said. "Why you whisperin'? Ain't nobody gonna hear you."

Brett shrugged his shoulders.

"Chad, you gonna look her straight in the eye?" Junior asked.

"Sure. I ain't afraid of the widow. Probably nothing under her veil anyway. She—"

"What's that?" Brett interrupted.

"I didn't hear nothin'," Junior said.

"Listen."

Chad heard it. The same eerie sound that he'd heard before. It gave him the goosebumps. He pulled at his suspenders.

"I heard it," Chad said stopping dead in his tracks. "It's comin' from the direction of the Foster place. Maybe we should—"

"Maybe we should what?" Junior asked.

"Nothin'," Chad said clearing his throat. "Let's go."

Chad, Brett, and Junior walked in silence until they arrived at the Foster place. Chad huddled with the other boys near the split-rail fence. The place looked empty except for some sheep in a nearby pen.

"Well...go," Junior urged Chad.

"Wait here." Chad swallowed hard. His throat felt as dry as an empty hay wagon. He slipped between the rails of the fence like a fox and crept slowly forward. He looked back to make sure the boys were still waiting for him. Then he heard the sound of horses approaching. Chad ran back to the fence and bolted over it. He didn't want anyone to catch him sneaking around.

"Hey, you there. What are you doing?" one of the soldiers called to Chad from the trail.

"Nothin'...nothin', sir," Chad answered.

"Been sneakin' around the Foster place?" the soldier asked. His brass buttons gleamed in the sun.

"No, sir. Ain't no reason to go there," Chad said. He rubbed his sweaty hands on his trousers.

The soldier stared at him. "No tellin' what might happen, if you get caught sneakin' around." The soldier stretched in his saddle. His horse snorted loudly. "Now, you best get along."

"Yes, sir," Chad said as he headed down the trail toward home.

Chad saw Junior and Brett take off like jackrabbits in the other direction. The soldiers from nearby Fort McKinney galloped away.

Chad sighed. Even the soldiers knew enough to stay away from the Foster place. At least for now, he wouldn't have to look anyone in the eye.

Chapter 4
Get Out!

"You still plannin' to pay a visit to the widow Foster after school?" Junior asked Chad the next morning.

"I don't know. Maybe it's not such a good idea. Remember what the soldier said. No tellin' what—"

"Chickenin' out, Chad?"

Chad lifted his straw hat and scratched his head. "I reckon not. I told you I'd do it."

"We're countin' on you. Aren't we, Brett?"

"Yep. Don't want to let your friends down, do you?"

After school the boys returned to the Foster place. Chad wondered how he had ever gotten into this mess. If only he'd kept his mouth shut. Why couldn't he just walk away?

"You see anythin'?" Brett asked Chad.

"No."

"Maybe you should just walk up to her door."

"You crazy or somethin', Brett?"

Chad knelt quietly behind a clump of willows. Junior and Brett knelt next to him. A swarm of gnats hovered over his head. The late afternoon sun warmed the back of his neck. Chad could feel sweat form on his forehead as he searched the Foster's yard with his eyes.

The little boy with the white hair came from around the side of the cabin. His head rocked back and forth. He appeared to be singing to himself.

"Jesse. Come here," a woman's voice called from inside the cabin.

Jesse must be the little boy's name, Chad thought to himself. He seemed so strange.

"At least we know she's in the cabin. Why don't you sneak up to the window and peek in?" Junior told Chad.

"What if she sees me? I'll get a whippin' if my father finds out."

"She won't see you if you're careful. Besides, she doesn't even know who you are, and she doesn't talk to folks anyway."

Junior nudged Chad forward. Chad looked over his shoulder at Junior and Brett. He had to do it.

"You gonna wait here?" Chad asked wiping his sweaty hands on his trousers.

"Sure," Junior assured him. "Now get."

Chad stepped away from the clump of willows into the open. He climbed over the split-rail fence. His feet touched the dry ground making a puff of dust rise. He hesitated for a moment and then approached the cabin.

Chokecherry bushes surrounded the run-down cabin. As he got closer the smell of cooked cabbage tickled his nose. Sheep bleated in a nearby pen. He ducked down beneath the front window and began to raise himself up so he could peek in the window.

The Black Widow had her back to him. She stirred a black iron pot that spit boiling water onto the dirt floor.

Suddenly, Chad felt somebody tug at his trouser leg. He heard heavy breathing. He turned his head quickly around and looked down. A pair of innocent blue eyes met his eyes. The strange little boy with white hair and runny nose stared into Chad's face. Jesse. Chad studied the expression on the boy's face. He stood up without thinking.

"Get out!" screamed an angry voice from inside the cabin. "Get out! You've no right sneakin' about my place."

Chad's feet suddenly felt heavy like a sack of wheat and he couldn't move. His heart pounded like a herd of buffalo. He had to get away, but he couldn't move. Jesse's eyes opened wide.

"Get out I said!"

"Mama! What's wrong?" Aubrey yelled from behind the cabin.

When Chad heard Aubrey's voice he turned around. His feet raced forward like a jackrabbit. Chad's straw hat blew off his head and landed behind him. He couldn't stop now. He wouldn't.

Chad vaulted over the rail fence and hurried toward the trail. Junior and Brett followed after him. The widow angrily shook her fist at Chad from her yard.

"Leave us alone!" she warned.

Chad slowed down when he reached the bend in the trail. An eerie childlike scream faded behind him.

"Well, did you see her face? What did she look like?" Junior demanded to know.

"Did you see her face?" Brett asked out of breath.

Junior and Brett desperately wanted to know what he had seen. Chad opened his mouth, then paused. His throat felt like a dry sand bed. Maybe he should lie, tell them her face looked like a buffalo with dark, evil eyes. No. He wouldn't lie.

"I didn't see her face."

"What! You looked right in the window," Junior shouted.

"I couldn't see her face. She had her back toward me."

"Can't you do anything right?" Junior complained.

"Like to see you do it, Junior," Chad mumbled to himself.

Chad watched Junior and Brett disappear around the bend before he headed home. He decided to ask his mother about the widow.

He stopped along the way home to pick some blue wildflowers growing near the trail. Flowers would make his mother feel happy.

Chad guessed that his mother tired of praire life. She worked hard from morning till night. He'd seen her crying at the end of many a day.

His 2-year-old sister, Becky, became sick and died on the Oregon Trail just before the wagon train reached Scott's Bluff, Nebraska. That happened 2 years ago, but it still hurt Chad and his mom like a bad cut that heals slowly and scars. The mention of his sister's name brought tears to her eyes.

Chad remembered how his father buried Becky along the trail, the day after his friend Clint died. His mother wept bitterly for Becky. Pa cried too. Chad bit his lip and held back the tears. He missed Becky.

"Ma," Chad called as he entered the front yard. "Ma, where are you?"

"I'm over here in the garden."

"Ma, I brought you some flowers."

"Oh they're lovely." She took the flowers from Chad and held them up to her nose. Ma closed her eyes and sniffed. Then she placed her hand on Chad's shoulder. "You're such a thoughtful boy. They're lovely," she repeated. "Thank you."

After his mother had placed the flowers in a tin cup of water, she went back to the garden. She was planting potatoes. His mother planned to sell potatoes to the soldiers at Fort McKinney, if she had a good crop. Chad helped her.

"Ma, do you know anythin' about widow Foster?"

"Well," she paused, "I saw her once in town. She wore this black veil over her face, like she was hidin' somethin'. I spoke to her in front of the courthouse, said good mornin' or somethin'. She just nodded her head and kept right on walkin'. Why do you ask?"

"Just wonderin'."

"Sometimes wonderin' can get you into a heap of trouble. It's none of our business what the widow does. Let her be. Besides, I hear some folks think she's evil."

"Ma, sometimes you can hear terrible sounds comin' from the Foster place."

"Is that so? Best you stay away from there," his mother warned. "By the way, where's your hat?"

"I must have left it at school," Chad said quickly. He didn't want to lie, but he didn't want a whipping either.

After supper Chad asked his father what he knew about the widow Foster.

"Reckon I don't know much. I know she raises sheep. Some of the ranchers don't take kindly to that. There's another article in the *Big Horn Sentinel* this week about the trouble brewin' between the cattlemen and the sheepherders," his father said.

"Surely a few sheep can't do any harm," his mother added as she cleared the table.

"This here's cattle country," his father said. "Lots of folks think that way."

"What do you think, Pa?"

"I reckon there's enough land for everybody, but right or wrong not everyone agrees."

Chapter 5

A Promise

The next day Aubrey stood waiting by the front school steps with Chad's hat. Chad looked around to see whether Junior and Brett had come to school yet. He couldn't see them so he walked toward Aubrey.

"Mama says I should give this back to you," Aubrey said. She stared directly into Chad's eyes. "She says you'd better leave us alone, or else."

Chad blushed like a prairie fire. Or else, he thought to himself. He swallowed hard.

"Thanks," he said taking the tattered hat from her small hand.

The bell rang and Aubrey headed up the steps to the schoolhouse. Chad followed her like a puppy that had been caught chewing a new boot. He wanted to apologize, but he couldn't.

Later that day Miss Bryant talked to the children about the forty-niners' rush west to find gold in California. She asked the class what the word treasure meant. Aubrey told the class that she had a treasure.

"Ruby freckles," Junior blurted out.

"James Junior. How rude," Miss Bryant scolded. "You apologize this instant."

"Sorry."

"You may stay after school and write 'I will be kind to others' 25 times."

"But, Miss Bryant."

"Don't you Miss Bryant me."

"Yes, ma'am."

Brett began to chuckle.

"Would you like to join him, Brett Thomas?"

"No, ma'am."

"Now, where were we? Oh yes. Aubrey, you said you have a treasure. Can you tell us more about it?" Miss Bryant asked.

"I can't, Miss Bryant," Aubrey said looking down at her faded brown dress.

Some children began to giggle and others whispered. Aubrey hung her head and tugged at her braid. Chad felt sorry for her.

Chad walked home by himself after school. He made sure he stayed behind Aubrey. If he caught up with her, he'd have to apologize. What would he say? He'd better leave her alone.

Aubrey turned off the trail toward her cabin. Chad hurried past the Foster's place. He had safely passed by it, when he heard Aubrey scream. She screamed again.

Chad wondered what to do. Should he dare to find out what was wrong? Aubrey screamed louder. Chad jumped over the split-rail fence and raced into the yard. Aubrey knelt by the woodpile. The woodpile had fallen on Aubrey's mother. Only the back of her head and an arm extended loose from under the pile of firewood.

"Help me! Please help me!" Aubrey pleaded.

Chad began to lift the wood off the widow. He tried not to make anymore wood fall on her. Aubrey held her mother's hand tightly.

"You'll be all right, Mama. You'll be all right." Aubrey turned to Chad. "Hurry, please hurry."

The widow had been knocked out, but her eyes began to flutter open.

"Aubrey, what happened? Who's that?"

"Chad. He helped us, Mama. It's all right."

Chad couldn't see the widow's face. She tried to move.

"Wait! Let me get the rest of the wood off you," Chad said.

Chad and Aubrey helped her mother stand up. She looked away from Chad. Then she slowly turned and looked him in the eye. Chad gasped. One side of her face twisted like melted butter left in the sun. Red skin draped over her cheekbone and her eye drooped. She had no eyelashes or eyebrow.

Chad felt sick to his stomach. He wanted to run away, but he couldn't. He just stared.

"Are you all right?" Chad finally managed to ask. He wiped his sweaty hands on his trousers.

"I'll be just fine," she said sharply. "Luckily nothin's broken. I should be more careful."

The widow stared back at Chad. He felt uneasy.

"You're that boy with the straw hat. The one who was nosin' around yesterday," the widow said brushing herself off.

"Yes, Ma'am." Chad wiped the sweat from his brow.

"Well, now you've seen my face. What do you think?"

"Mama, don't!"

Chad stared at Aubrey. He continued to wipe his hands on his trousers. He wanted to speak, but his throat dried up like the prairie grasses in summer.

"I suppose I should be thankin' you for bein' neighborly and helpin'," the widow sighed.

"I-I-I better go now," Chad stammered.

"You won't tell anyone about what you saw? I don't want people starin' and pointin' at me like I was some kind of freak."

"Oh no, ma'am. I-I-I won't tell anyone."

"Promise."

Chad crossed his heart. He wanted to get out of there. He wanted to ask what happened to her face, but he was scared. Then he felt a pat on his back. Chad saw the little boy with the white hair smiling up at him. He seemed so small and helpless.

"Jesse," Chad said softly. Chad knelt next to him. Jesse reached out his arms to hug him. Chad hesitated, then hugged Jesse close and tight, like he used to hold his sister, Becky. It felt good, warm, and loving.

"You help Mama," Jesse said with a big smile.

Chad smiled back at Jesse. Jesse's eyes twinkled.

The widow studied Chad and Jesse together.

"He likes you," she said.

He likes me, Chad thought to himself. No, I can't—not again, not after losing Becky. I don't ever want to hurt like that again.

"I'd better go," Chad said.

"Remember! You promised," the widow reminded him.

Chad looked back over his shoulder. Jesse waved happily. He could still picture Becky waving to him. He had to forget how good it felt to hug Jesse.

Now Chad knew why the widow hid her face. What terrible thing could have happened to her?

Chad walked out of sight of the cabin, when he heard that eerie sound again. Sounds like a child. No. It couldn't be. What else was the widow hiding?

Chapter 6
A Secret

"*How is your mama?*" the note read. Aubrey looked over at Chad, then she wrote, "*good,*" on her slate board.

Chad smiled and nodded his head. The little girl sitting behind Chad raised her hand.

"Miss Bryant," she said. "Chad and Aubrey are writin' love notes."

Junior looked up from his book and grinned at Chad. Chad felt his face glow like hot coals. He quickly wiped off his slate board, so that nobody could read it. He glared back at the little girl.

"Chad," Miss Bryant asked. "Are you writing notes?"

"Yes, ma'am. But not love notes."

"I'll talk to you and Aubrey after school."

When school was dismissed, Chad and Aubrey stepped up to Miss Bryant's desk. She scolded them for not paying attention to their lessons. Then she smiled and blamed the problem on "spring fever."

"Now scoot before you're missed," she said.

"May I walk with you?" Aubrey asked Chad as he left the room.

"Well, I suppose."

"Sorry I got you into trouble."

"It's nothin'."

Chad and Aubrey walked down the narrow trail together. The heavy stillness made Chad feel uneasy. He remembered the day before.

"Aubrey, what makes those awful cries at your place?"

Aubrey twirled the end of her rusty braid with her finger.

"I can't tell, or I'll get into trouble. It's a secret. Mama says I shouldn't tell nobody."

Chad studied her face for a moment. "It's your little brother, isn't it? It's Jesse."

"No. It's not Jesse."

Chad waited for Aubrey to say more. He walked in silence. The smell of horses filtered through the trees, and a deer fly buzzed above Chad's head. Chad slapped at the fly, but he missed.

"Promise not to tell anyone what I tell you?" Aubrey took a deep breath.

"Sure. I promise."

"Cross your heart."

"Cross my heart. Besides, I didn't tell anyone about your ma's face, did I?"

"Well," Aubrey paused. "Mama and I have a treasure hidden behind the cabin. It's our secret, but maybe she'll let me tell you. I trust you. I'll ask her tonight."

"Sure," Chad said with a curious look.

Chad and Aubrey walked quietly together. Only the sound of a horsefly broke the silence.

"Tell me about Jesse."

Aubrey's face looked sad, but then she smiled. "Jesse loves everythin', especially the meadowlarks. We play together when my chores are done. Jesse laughs a lot, but he isn't well. He has trouble breathin' sometimes. Scares me."

"Is he smart like you?"

Aubrey smiled at Chad. Chad felt his face turn red. He rubbed his hands on his trousers.

"Jesse's not school smart," Aubrey said. "He learns slowly, but Mama says he knows more about love. Says that's more important than book learnin'. Says that—"

Chad placed his hand in front of Aubrey to stop her. He froze in the dusty trail. Aubrey didn't move. They stood silent and motionless like chunks of granite. Only the deer fly dared to move. A large snake slithered across the trail in front of him. Chad thought it looked like a rattlesnake. Bull snakes looked like rattlers. Unsure, Chad waited until the snake disappeared in the grass by the side of the trail.

"I didn't see it," Aubrey said. "Thanks."

The fine brown hairs on Chad's arm stood on end.

"I hate snakes, especially rattlers," Chad admitted.

"Me too. Chad, come see Jesse again. He likes you."

"I don't know. Maybe."

Chad and Aubrey said goodby at the end of the trail. Chad heard an awful sound as Aubrey disappeared behind the trees. What could it be? Maybe he'd find out on Monday.

"Where'd your sweetheart go?" Junior appeared from behind some bushes.

Chad jumped in surprise. He thought he was alone.

"What are you doin' here?"

"Brett and I decided to follow you and your sweetheart."

"Aubrey's not my sweetheart. She's...nobody."

"Did she tell you about her evil mother?"

"She's not evil. At least I don't think so."

"How do you know? Have you talked to her?" Junior asked.

"Well, kind of...it's none of your business anyway."

"I make it my business."

"I have to go home and do chores. Pa's waitin'."

Junior and Brett blocked Chad's way. Junior shoved Chad.

"Tell me what's goin' on at the Foster place, or I'll punch your face in."

"Nothin'! I don't know nothin'."

"You do to."

"I told you. I don't know nothin'."

"You liar," Junior said as he punched Chad in the mouth.

Chad fell backward into the dust. His lip split open like a cracked tomato. He touched his lip with his finger and stared at the blood on it. If only he wasn't so afraid, he'd...but he was. He stood and ran toward home. He looked back once to see Junior and Brett laughing.

"You're a snake, James Junior!"

Chapter 7

Not Like Pa

Saturday morning Chad and his mother took the buckboard wagon into town to pick up supplies. His mother sold eggs to the general store. The hens had started laying heavily, and so his mother had a large basketful. Chad hoped there might be extra money for some candy.

A light rain during the night had settled the dust on the wagon trail, making travel more pleasant. A gentle southern wind brushed the smells of early spring over the countryside. Towering mountain peaks glistened white to the west.

"Ma. Peppermint sticks sure would taste good."

"Would they?"

"Yes, ma'am. Nothin' better than peppermint sticks."

"Better than my homemade pie?"

"Oh no, Ma. Nothin' better than your pie."

Chad's mother laughed at him. "You're just like your pa."

Chad liked to hear that. Just like his pa. His thoughts drifted up into the web of wispy white clouds above. What would his pa think about the widow if he'd seen her? Would he like Jesse and be his friend? Pa had a kind heart.

He remembered the time in Ohio when Pa gave the neighbors a cow after their barn burned down. He never would take any money for it. Then there was the time his pa rescued a boy who was being chased by a gang of older boys. One time he made a man apologize to a lady for being rude.

No, he wasn't like his pa. Pa wouldn't let Junior pick on Aubrey. "It's not right," he'd say. But he wasn't big and strong like Pa. What could he do? He wasn't like his pa.

"Chad, what's wrong?"

"Nothin'. Just thinkin'."

Chad and his mother drove the team of horses up the dusty curving main street of Buffalo, Wyoming. The small cattle town bordered the Bozeman Trail. It was nestled between the Big Horn foothills and the prairie.

Chad and his mother waved to Sarah Buell in front of the Occidental Hotel as they passed by. Loud laughter came from the saloon as the horses plodded toward the J. H. Conrad & Company General Store. The general store stood facing the mountains to the west. Chad could see snow-covered peaks shimmering from the store front. He looked to see whether the Clearmont stagecoach had departed yet. No sign of it.

After tying up the team in front of the general store, Chad stepped up onto the wooden sidewalk and hurried inside. The general store had so much to see. Canned goods lined the shelves. Bolts of brightly colored calico and gingham covered the counters. Jars of penny candy begged to be eaten. Traps hung on the walls along with cast iron kettles, coffee pots, and fur pelts. A large pickle barrel sat under the front window.

Chad's mother needed to buy some salt pork, flour, and lace trim. Chad walked over to a collection of store bought hats.

"I'd sure like a new hat," he said softly to himself.

"Would you?" a voice said from behind the cracker barrel.

Chad turned around to see Junior pop out from behind the barrel. He wore a smirk on his chubby face.

"Scare you?" Junior teased.

"I didn't see you."

"I know. Maybe you need to watch out. Never know who's watchin' you."

Chad looked down at his boots. If only Junior would leave him alone. Junior snickered and left the store. Chad walked to where his mother stood looking at some lace.

"Which do you like better? I like this one," she said delicately tracing the lace with her rough fingertips."

"I reckon it will do fine," Chad said.

"Then I'll get this one," she said and walked to the counter to pay the clerk.

"Looks like your ma's gettin' ready for somethin' special," the clerk said. "This wouldn't have anythin' to do with Wyoming becomin' a state, would it?"

Chad grinned. His mother smiled.

"July 10th is going to be a day to remember," his mother told the clerk. "Imagine, the Wyoming Territory becomin' the 44th state of the Union."

"Yep," said the clerk. "It's gonna be some celebration."

"Ma, suppose I could have some candy?"

"I reckon."

"Thanks, Ma."

Chad picked out some peppermint sticks. He placed one in his pocket for something special and began eating the other. The candy sweetened his whole mouth. He closed his eyes for a moment and savored the taste.

"I wish I could have candy all the time."

"If you had it all the time, maybe it wouldn't taste so good," his mother said.

Chad saw the widow enter the store. He suddenly felt weak.

"What's the matter, Chad?" his mother asked. "You look awfully pale." His mother turned to see the widow. When the widow saw Chad she stopped.

"Mornin'," Chad managed to say.

"Mornin', Mrs. Foster," his mother said politely.

The widow stood motionless for a moment. Then she pulled the black spidery veil closer to her face. She nodded a greeting and went about her business.

Chad and his mother left the store. He glanced back, but the widow never looked his way.

"Strange," his mother said as the buckboard headed out of town. "The way the widow acted. Wonder why?"

"May...maybe she thought we were somebody else," Chad said.

"I suppose, but it seems strange. Are you all right?"

"I'm all right," Chad said.

"Well anyway, I'm glad I bought the lace for my dress. I want to look my best for your pa. He and I are gonna dance up a storm to celebrate the statehood."

Chad knew the statehood celebration would be grand. There would be dancing and singing, pie-eating contests, and races. There would be plenty of cakes and pies to eat, and maybe a new hat. Ma would wear her new dress trimmed with lace, and Pa would play his fiddle. Maybe he could enter the three legged race with Brett. July 10th seemed so far away, but he knew 1890 would be a year he'd never forget.

Chad's thoughts wandered back to the widow. Maybe he should have pretended not to see her. Was she afraid he would say something about her face? At least she hadn't called him by his name.

In the back of his mind he heard the eerie cries coming from the Foster place. It gave him the goosebumps. He pulled at his suspenders. Did he really want to know Aubrey's secret? Like Ma said, "Sometimes not knowin' is better."

Chapter 8
Trust Me

After school Chad and Aubrey raced home to see the treasure. Aubrey wouldn't tell Chad what it was.

Chad nervously played with his suspenders as he followed Aubrey behind the Foster cabin. Chokecherry trees hid the place where the treasure must be kept. A loud catlike sound made Chad stop.

"Don't be afraid," Aubrey said. "Now close your eyes and take my hand. Trust me."

Chad didn't want to hold her hand, but he did. She brought Chad to a shed with a pen connected to it.

"Open your eyes," she said.

Chad opened his eyes and stared in amazement at the surprise before him. It made that eerie sound that had frightened him.

"What is it?"

"It's a peacock. Mama's peacock. Pa gave it to her just before...," Aubrey's voice faded away.

"Before what?"

Aubrey started to tell him, but she stopped. Someone was coming.

"I've never seen a peacock. What do you call it?"

"Precious," a voice said from behind Chad.

Chad turned to see the widow standing there. The scarring on the side of her face turned away from him.

"Aubrey, what did I tell you?" she scolded.

"I know, but Chad's my friend and I just had to tell someone. Don't be mad, Mama."

"I-I-I won't tell anyone," Chad stammered.

"You'd better not! I don't want anyone stealing him for his feathers."

"Precious is very special to me." The widow stared at the bird and smiled a half-twisted smile. Chad thought it was a sad smile. For the first time he felt sorry for her.

Chad watched the peacock. Its fantail shone brilliantly in the sun. The glint of gold in the feathers blended with rich indigo and turquoise danced in the light. The large bird strutted proudly around the dusty pen. It sounds almost human, Chad thought to himself.

"Aubrey, you need to do your chores. I'll be needin' help in the garden too."

"I can help," Chad blurted out.

"No need to. We can manage."

"I don't mind. I like workin' in the garden. I always help my ma."

The widow studied Chad for a moment. "All right," she agreed. "My brother, Frank, said he'd be back in the spring to help plant. Reckon he's still got gold fever. He promised I could stay here if I kept up the place. More work than I figured on though." The widow brushed a long wisp of hair away from her face.

Chad hoed deep furrows as the widow planted the seed potatoes. She didn't say much. Chad talked about the weather and his mother's garden. He tried not to look at her face. Jesse followed him down the rows giving him a hug now and then. He had to admit he was beginning to like Jesse. When the seed potatoes had been nestled snuggly into the earth, Chad asked to stay and play with Jesse. The widow said that Jesse would like that.

"Bird," Jesse said pointing to a meadowlark perched on a fence post. "Bird," he repeated.

"Jesse loves meadowlarks," Aubrey said.

Chad played tag with Jesse and twirled him around in wavy circles. He put Jesse on his knee and played horsey. Jesse giggled and giggled. Aubrey laughed at the two boys. Chad noticed the sun had disappeared and looked up into the sky. Dark, angry clouds covered the horizon.

"I'd better go," he told Aubrey. "Ma will be wonderin' about me." Chad pulled his hat down tight on his head. He flinched as a vein of lightning tore into the blackish skin of sky. "Give me a hug, Jesse."

"Thanks for helpin'," the widow said. "Best you be gettin' home."

"See you," Aubrey said waving goodby.

Chad waved goodby to the Fosters and hurried down the trail. Thunder rumbled across the mountains. Then he noticed Junior and Brett waiting by the roadside. Not again, he thought to himself.

"Looky here, Brett," Junior exclaimed. "It's the Black Widow's new boy," Junior laughed.

Chad tried to walk around the boys, but they stopped him.

"What's goin' on at the Foster place? We saw you helpin' in the garden and playin' with that strange little kid."

"He's not strange. I like him."

"You like him?" Brett snickered.

"I didn't ask you," Chad said clenching his fist.

Another flash of lightning and a sharp crack of thunder made Chad jump. A cold drop of rain poked his face.

"I think she's put a spell on you. I saw you go behind the cabin with Aubrey and her mother. Heard those creepy sounds. What did she do to you?" Junior glared at Chad.

Chad pulled on his suspenders. "I'm not under any spell. Aubrey showed me her..." Chad bit his lip.

"Her what?" Junior wanted to know.

"Nothin'."

A brilliant flash of light and an instant crash of thunder ended the talk. A nearby cottonwood tree splintered in half. Chad jumped in fright.

"I'm gettin' out of here!" Brett shouted.

"I...I best be gettin' too. My pa needs my help," Junior said backing off.

Junior and Brett raced home. Chad wondered what to do now. He'd opened his big mouth again. Junior would try to make him talk.

The rain pelted Chad as he charged home. He wanted to shut out the lightning that weaved itself into the dull gray sky. If only he could blot out the sound of the thunder. It all reminded him of the terrible night on the wagon train—the night Becky died.

Chapter 9

Hang On!

The next day stormy clouds masked the mountains at the prairie's edge. The swollen stream licked at the banks like angry flames. Miss Bryant sent the children home early because of the chance of a flash flood. There would be no warning.

Chad remembered stories about flash floods. One story told how a wagon train had been swallowed by a raging stream. High mountain rains caused a flash flood in the valley below, where the wagon train was circled. The sun shone in a burning blue sky, when the water surprised the wagon train. A thunderous roar, like a herd of stampeding buffalo, was the only warning. Half the people on the train drowned.

"I saw you talking to Junior and Brett," Aubrey said. "Did you tell them?"

"No. I promised, didn't I? Don't you trust me?"

"I trust you, but I know what Junior is like."

"Don't worry. I won't tell," Chad said. He smiled at Aubrey. "We'd better hurry home."

Chad and Aubrey were almost to the Foster place when he heard a thunderous sound.

"Listen," he said. "Do you hear it?"

"Yes."

Chad looked at Aubrey. A rumbling sound grew louder and louder.

"Run, Aubrey! Climb a tree!"

"I'm scared." Aubrey's face scrunched up in fear. "I can't swim."

Chad grabbed Aubrey's arm and pulled her away from the trail that bordered the creek. He headed toward a large cottonwood tree. He ordered Aubrey to start climbing.

"I can't!"

"You have to. Now climb!" Chad said giving her a push.

Aubrey tried to pull herself up, but her arms were weak.

"I can't!" she cried. "I can't!"

"You have to. Pull!" Chad shouted, pushing her from behind. The roar of water raged louder. A muddy wall of water crashed down the creek bed and spilled over onto the trail. The dirty water churned like rapids, smacking its greedy lips at the base of the tree. Chad pushed his hat down tight.

"It's getting closer, Aubrey. Climb! Hurry!"

Aubrey pulled herself up. Chad followed behind her, but the water began tearing at his legs. The water grabbed his body with tremendous force.

Chad held on to the tree trunk with all his might. If he let go, he would be swept away like a fallen leaf.

Aubrey clung to the tree like a vine just above Chad. Her eyes opened wide with fright.

"Hold on, Chad. Don't let go," she pleaded.

"I don't know if I can!"

The turbulent water pulled at him like a robin pulling a worm out of the ground. He wrapped his arms around the trunk of the tree. His body twisted and shook as the water tried to carry him away. His legs ached from the cold. How long could he hold on?

"Hang on!" Aubrey shouted above the water's roar.

"Oh, Aubrey, I'm so scared," Chad cried. "I don't want to die."

Chad's arms ached and he began to cry.

"Help!" he yelled in desperation. "Help me!"

Then the water began to recede, swirling away, almost as fast as it had risen. The foul water gave up and released Chad. He rested his legs on a branch. He wasn't going to die.

"Are you all right?" Aubrey asked.

"I'm all right? I did it, Aubrey. I held on. I was scared, but I held on." Chad smiled for Aubrey. He shook from the cold, but he felt good inside. He was alive.

When it was safe, Chad and Aubrey climbed down from the tree.

"It's over," Chad sighed.

"What about Mama and Jesse? Do you think—"

Chad and Aubrey ran down the trail to the Foster place. Aubrey's mother greeted her with open arms.

"I'm so glad you're safe," Aubrey's mother said. "I could see the flooding from here, and I was afraid for you."

"Mama, Chad saved my life! He heard the flood water comin' and he made me climb a tree. He made me, Mama. He saved my life!"

Chad blushed. He hadn't thought about it.

"I reckon I owe you," the widow said. "That's the second time you've helped us."

Chad didn't know what to say. He tugged at his wet suspenders.

"Wait here," Aubrey's mother said. "I have somethin' for you."

The widow went into the cabin and returned with a peacock feather.

"I want you to have this. Don't tell anyone where you got it," she warned.

Chad took the feather from her hand. All the beautiful colors of Precious were in this one feather.

"Thanks, ma'am."

"You best get home and put on some dry clothes," the widow suggested. "You'll catch a death of cold."

"Hug," Jesse said from behind. "Hug."

"You bet."

Chad picked up Jesse and hugged him tight. Then he twirled Jesse around until Jesse giggled.

"Bird," Jesse said. "Pretty."

"Pretty. Very pretty," Chad repeated with a smile. "Oh, I almost forgot. This is for you."

Chad pulled out a peppermint stick from his pocket for Jesse. It was wet and sticky. The red-and-white swirls had blended to pink from the water. Jesse stared at it.

"It's candy. Yum," Chad said and pretended to eat some.

Jesse tasted the candy and lit up like a firefly.

"Yum," Jesse said. "Yum, yum, yum, yum!"

Chad began to shiver and so he said goodby. He hurried home to get some dry clothes. His mother greeted him in the yard.

"I was just about to send your father out to find you. I've been so worried," his mother said with a big hug.

Chad changed into some dry clothes and sat by the fire to get warm. His mother made him some hot tea to drink. Chad told her all about the flood and how he had found this beautiful feather near the Foster place.

"You still hangin' around there?" his mother asked. "Why do you keep goin' over there anyway? You and that little girl, are you friends?"

"Yea, I guess we are. Besides, the widow is all right. You just have to get to know her. Her little boy, Jesse, and I are friends. He giggles a lot."

"No harm in that, I reckon. It's a joy to have a young'un around. Like my Beck..." Chad's mother stopped. She wrapped her arms around herself and stared off toward the prairie. Her face tightened and her shoulders sagged. She lowered her head and her eyes moistened with tears.

"Don't cry, Mama. I miss Becky too." Chad put his arm around his mother's shoulder.

"Ma," Chad said trying to change the subject, "I got a secret. Me and Aubrey and her mother..."

"What?" his mother said looking at Chad.

"I said...oh nothin'."

Just then his father returned from the range and rode his horse into the yard.

Chad decided he'd better not say anymore. The secret had gotten him into enough trouble already. Instead he gave his mother a hug. He was alive.

Chapter 10

Missing Treasure

"I hear you like Aubrey Foster," Junior teased from in front of the schoolhouse. Miss Bryant rang the school bell.

"I do not!" Chad cried above the clang of the bell.

"You're wearin' a mighty big smile this mornin'. Looks like a love smile to me."

"Am not." Chad could feel the muscles tighten in his jaw.

"Did the Black Widow put another spell on you?"

Chad decided not to let Junior get the best of him on such a fine morning. He thought for a moment.

"Maybe. If you're not careful, I'll have her put a spell on you."

Chad tipped his hat and told Junior and Brett to step aside.

Later that day Junior told Chad that he and Brett would find out the widow's secret. Chad warned Aubrey to be careful.

Chad thought Aubrey might like to see the new kittens in the barn. He invited her to come home with him. Aubrey figured it would be all right, since her mother had gone into town for supplies.

He and Aubrey didn't have to search far to find the kittens. In the corner of the empty stall, his gray tiger cat lazily nursed a litter of four kittens. The cat stretched comfortably as the babies nursed. The cat purred loud and steady as Chad stroked her.

Two of the kittens were gray tigers like the mother. One kitten was black and shiny like coal, and the other kitten was a golden yellow.

"I like this one," Aubrey said gently picking up the yellow mewing tuft of fur. "It kind of reminds me of Jesse. It must be the color."

"Think your mama would let you have one."

"Maybe. She likes cats. We could use a good mouser. I chase mice with a broom in the cabin."

"I hate mice. They give me the creeps," Chad admitted.

"I think mice are cute, but they do make a mess in the cupboard."

"You mean, you're not afraid of mice?" Chad said in surprise.

"Of course not."

He scratched his head. Chad thought all girls were afraid of mice.

Chad and Aubrey left for the Foster place to see the peacock. The sky darkened with storm clouds again. Chad could hear the rumble of thunder already rolling over the foothills.

"I told Miss Bryant about Precious. Mama said I could probably trust Miss Bryant."

"What did Miss Bryant say?"

"She said I was lucky to have such a treasure."

Chad and Aubrey found the gate to the peacock's pen ajar. There was no sign of Precious. Aubrey covered her face with her hands and cried.

"Don't worry, Aubrey. We'll find it," Chad assured her.

Chad heard the widow's wagon entering the yard. Aubrey rushed out to meet her mother.

"Mama!...Mama! Precious...Precious is gone!"

Aubrey's mother stepped down from the wagon. "What's wrong?" she asked pulling the long black veil away from her face.

"Precious is gone. Chad and I came home to see Precious and the gate was open. Oh, Mama! Where could he be?"

Aubrey's mother clutched at her throat and began searching the yard with her eyes. Then something caught her attention in a clump of dried weeds by the shed.

"Maybe that's him over there," she said running to the shed. "I see something. It's...it's a grouse." She gave a deep sigh as her shoulders sagged in disappointment.

The wind suddenly picked up and rain dampened Chad's face.

"Better head home, Chad. Storm's breakin'," the widow said. "Aubrey and I will look for Precious later.

I've got to get Jesse in out of the rain. I can't let him get chilled. We'll find him."

"But—"

"Get. Aubrey and I will find him."

Chad took off on a run.

The stormy weather continued all night. Lightning sizzled in the sky like bacon in a fry pan. Hail pelted the cabin, and pea-sized hail grew to marble size that covered the ground. Thunder from the giant cloud drums shook the cabin. Chad thought it would never end.

The next morning Chad left early for school. Crisp, fresh air filled his lungs. The wet cottonwoods glistened in the soft sunlight. The creek rushed full and strong. Hail laced the edge of the trail in someplaces like pearls. When he got to the Foster place, Aubrey greeted him at the door.

"Mama and I can't find Precious anywhere."

"Maybe we'll find him along the trail on our way to school," Chad said.

"Maybe."

Jesse ran out to give Chad a hug. "For you," he said.

He handed Chad a wilted wild violet. Jesse began to cough.

"Thanks, Jesse. It's pretty." He hugged Jesse again. "Did the storm scare you last night?"

Jesse nodded with melon-sized eyes.

"Me too," Chad whispered in his ear. "I've got to go now. Aubrey and I are going to look for Precious on our way to school."

Jesse began coughing again.

"Sounds like you're catchin' a cold, Jesse. Better get some rest."

Chad and Aubrey searched the roadside and looked for any sign of the peacock, but found nothing. When they reached the school, Miss Bryant had a worrisome look on her face. She asked Aubrey to follow her behind the schoolhouse. She said there was something Aubrey needed to see. Chad heard Aubrey scream and then watched as she ran away from the school.

"Wait! Aubrey, wait!" Miss Bryant called out to her.

Chad thought he should run after her, but the boys were watching. He didn't know what to do.

"What's wrong?" Chad asked Miss Bryant.

Miss Bryant held her hand over her mouth. She was about to speak, when Chad bolted to the back of the schoolhouse. He stepped back in surprise. The body of Precious lay dead on the grass. Its beautiful feathers wet and muddy.

"I found it near the schoolhouse this morning and dragged it back here. The hail must have killed it. Poor thing," the gentle voice of Miss Bryant said from behind him. She placed her hand on his shoulder. "It's Aubrey's treasure, isn't it?"

Chad felt his body stiffen in anger. Why?

"I'm so sorry," Miss Bryant said.

"If only the gate hadn't been left open," Chad said softly. "Who could have left the gate open? Could it have been Jesse?"

Chapter 11

It Still Hurts

The next morning Chad hurried to the Foster place to pick up Aubrey for school. He knocked on the door. Aubrey slowly opened the the cabin door. Her eyes looked red.

"Come in, Chad," Aubrey said.

"I...I brought you some feathers. I thought you'd like to keep them. Miss Bryant helped me bury Precious behind the schoolhouse." Chad handed the feathers to Aubrey. "I washed them in the creek and dried them by the fire last night. Are you all right?"

Aubrey stared at the feathers. "Poor Precious."

"Where's Jesse?"

"Come with me," Aubrey said.

Jesse was sick in bed. His mother sat on a stool next to him wiping his forehead with a damp cloth. She turned for a moment to look at Chad. Jesse started coughing.

"He's sick with fever," Jesse's mother sighed. "Pneumonia, I think. Started last night." She poured more water from a pitcher into a basin by Jesse's bedside. "Doc's out of town." She moistened the cloth and placed it on Jesse's forehead again. "Poor boy's always gettin' sick. Almost lost him twice."

Only Jesse's head could be seen from beneath the woolen blanket. His little body trembled and his cheeks burned red.

"Hug," Jesse said when he saw Chad. He breathed short, quick breaths. "Pesus all gone. Hug."

"Jesse loved Precious as much as I did," his mother said. "Can't imagine how the bird got loose."

Chad walked toward Jesse. The widow held up her hand to stop him.

"You best stay away," she said. "I don't want you gettin' sick too."

Chad stepped back. "I have to go to school."

"Hug," Jesse repeated. "Hug."

Aubrey grabbed Chad by the arm. "We'd better go. Bye, Jesse. Mama, you sure you don't want me to stay and help?"

"You get learnin'. I'll be fine."

"Sorry about Precious," Chad told Aubrey and her mother.

Chad and Aubrey walked slowly down the trail. Chad kicked a stone along the way. Aubrey twirled her bonnet strings with her finger.

"Mama loved that bird. Pa gave it to her the week before the fire," Aubrey exclaimed. "She's mighty upset about losing Precious and now Jesse is sick. Poor Mama."

"You had a fire?"

"The fire started late one night. Pa smelled smoke and woke up first. He told Mama to get out fast; then he climbed up to the loft and saved Jesse and me." Aubrey paused. Tears filled her eyes.

"What happened?"

"Pa ran back to save what he could. When he didn't come out right away, Ma ran back into the fire. The flames were everywhere by then. I remember how awful the smoke was. Poor Jesse was so scared. Suddenly, I heard Ma scream and she burst through the door. A burning timber fell on her." Aubrey brushed away a tear. "Pa never came out."

"So that's what happened to your ma's face."

Aubrey nodded. "She used to be real pretty. Pa said she looked like her name."

"What's her name?" Chad wondered.

"Rose...Rose Marie. Now she hides her face from people with that ugly black veil. Makes her look scary. People act as if my ma is some kind of freak and she isn't. She's sweet and kind. Ma takes good care of Jesse and me."

"After the fire, Ma wanted to get away. She wrote Uncle Frank. He said we could stay at his place, if we took care of it. That's how we ended up here along the creek."

Chad didn't know what to say. He walked on in silence for a while. Aubrey had been hurt too.

"Aubrey, does it still hurt? I mean...you know about your pa."

"I thought I would die at first, but I didn't. I still had Ma and Jesse. It hurts, but...well, I just try to remember the good things about Pa."

"I know what you mean," Chad said pulling hard on his suspenders.

"You do?"

"I never told you before, but I had a little sister. Her name was Becky. She was cute as a button, always singin' and laughin'."

"What happened to her?"

"She got sick and died. We were with the wagon train, so we buried her along the trail." Chad paused. "It still hurts. I said I'd never love a little kid like that again." Chad smiled. "But then I met Jesse."

"Jesse is sweet," Aubrey said.

Chad and Aubrey entered the schoolyard.

"I hope Jesse gets better," Aubrey said with a despairing look that made her appear older than she was.

"Hey everybody. Look! Here comes Chad and his sugar," Junior shouted.

Junior had not been at school yesterday and Chad hoped he would still be gone. He tried to ignore Junior.

"When you gonna get married?"

"Go away, Junior," Aubrey said walking away from him.

Chad followed her.

"You gonna chase after her or stay with the boys?" Junior taunted. "Make up your mind."

Chad blushed. He was afraid to leave Junior and follow his new friend. Then Junior began strutting around like a bird, a peacock.

Chad made up his mind. He would do the right thing, like his father. He wasn't going to be afraid anymore. Junior wasn't a real friend anyway.

"What are you doin', James Junior?" Chad demanded to know.

"Guess?" Junior began making strange sounds. Child-like, catlike sounds. Peacock sounds.

"You're the one. You let Precious loose." Chad clenched his fists and walked toward Junior. Junior stepped back.

"So what if I did?" Junior said.

"Why? What has Aubrey or her mother ever done to you?"

Chad stood right in front of Junior. Junior puffed up like a bullfrog and shoved Chad.

"Come on," Junior said punching Chad in the stomach.

That did it. Chad felt a rush of anger. It rose from his gut and into his arm. He pulled back his arm and punched Junior with all his might. Junior fell to the ground like a sack of grain. He looked stunned. Chad held back a second blow as he stood over Junior like an angry bear. The other children cheered.

"Don't you ever say nothin' bad about the widow, Aubrey, or Jesse again! You leave them alone. You hear?" Chad warned. "They're better than you. Understand?"

"All right. All right," Junior agreed.

Miss Bryant had been watching unnoticed from the door of the schoolhouse. "Boys, stop that!" she scolded and seemed to wipe away a smile.

Chad glared at the bully lying on the ground. Junior didn't seem all that big lying there.

"What's going on here?" Miss Bryant wanted to know.

Aubrey stepped forward like an angry hen ready to attack.

"Junior let Precious loose and now he's dead," Aubrey said kicking at Junior.

"Stop that, Aubrey. It won't bring Precious back," Miss Bryant said.

"I hate you, James Junior," Aubrey shouted.

Miss Bryant stared at Junior. "Look at me, James Junior. Did you let Aubrey's pet peacock get loose?"

Junior stuck out his lower lip and nodded his head. "Brett did it too."

Brett lowered his head.

Miss Bryant sighed. "First, you'll apologize to Aubrey. And second, you can be sure that your folks will hear about this."

Chapter 12

Not Again

Sunlight glistened on the new leaves of the cottonwoods. The damp smell of freshly plowed earth sweetened the air. Meadowlarks greeted the morning with their happy song. Chad felt good inside, more like Pa. Junior would leave him alone today.

Chad knocked on the Foster's cabin door. "Aubrey. You ready to go?"

The door creaked open. Aubrey stood holding the door. Her eyes were red and swollen. Something must have happened.

"What's wrong?"

"He's dead. Jesse is dead." Aubrey started back into the cabin.

Chad felt weak. His chest seemed heavy. Aubrey's words stung like a wasp. He followed Aubrey blindly back

54

to where Aubrey's mother cradled the limp body of Jesse. Tears trickled over her scarred face as she rocked back and forth in silence.

Chad froze. Jesse, not Jesse. It couldn't be, not again. Not after Becky. A fly buzzed and landed on his hand, the only sound in the room. His mind went blank.

"Help me one more time," the widow said softly. "Jesse needs to be buried. The fever...last night. His breathin' ain't never been good." She paused. "I rocked him so many times when he was a baby and couldn't sleep because of his breathin'. But he always got better. Now, my baby is gone and he needs to be buried."

The widow stood up and laid Jesse's body gently on the bed. She walked toward a cedar chest in the corner of the room. She emptied its contents on to a table. Her ivory wedding dress slipped through her hands. She placed an old doll, a fine linen tablecloth, and some other pieces of her life quietly on a barrel next to the chest.

"The shovel is out back behind the shed," the widow said. "We'll bury him in the chest. My pa made it for me. Told me it would hold my dreams." She began to cry.

Chad stood by Jesse. He looked asleep. He wanted to give Jesse one last hug, but instead he touched his lifeless hand. It felt cold. Chad suddenly felt sick to his stomach and ran out of the room.

Chad and the widow carried the cedar chest to the hillside. He helped to bury his little friend in sight of the prairie, the endless prairie. The meadowlarks would sing over his grave forever.

When the last stone had been placed on the grave site, Chad stood back. Jesse's mother placed a handful of blue larkspur at the base of the grave. Aubrey placed some yellow flowers next to them. Chad took the peacock feather out of his hat. Today was the first day he had worn it. He placed the feather by the flowers.

"Bye, Jesse," he whispered.

The widow placed her arm around Aubrey's shoulder. They started to walk toward the cabin. Chad followed. He wondered whether Becky and Jesse were together now. Becky would like Jesse.

"Thank you," Aubrey's mother said touching Chad's cheek. "Thank you for caring. You were Jesse's only friend."

Chad suddenly felt as if his heart had been torn apart. It wasn't fair. An icy emptiness seeped deep inside him. First Becky. Then Jesse. He fell to his knees and pounded the earth with his fists. Like hot coals hidden by ash, his anger burned. Now in a rage it flared.

"Why...Why...Why?" Chad cried out. "It's not fair. I loved Becky. I loved Jesse. How could it have happened twice?" A rush of tears filled his eyes. He began to sob uncontrollably.

The widow knelt next to Chad and held him tight. She rocked him as she had Jesse. Chad cried and cried.

"It hurts so bad," Chad said.

"I know...I know," the widow whispered.

"How can you stand it?" Chad asked wiping away the tears with the back of his hand. "You've lost your husband and now Jesse."

"It hurts, but a body has to carry on."

"I don't know if I can," Chad said.

"You will. You're young and you have your whole life ahead of you."

"But, what about you? What will you do?"

"I'm thinkin' maybe Aubrey and I should head back East. I got family back in Missouri. Aubrey deserves better than what we got here." The widow stood up and folded her hands to her chest. "You best get on to school. Tell Miss Bryant, Aubrey won't be comin' no more."

When Chad arrived at school it was almost noon. He walked quietly to Miss Bryant's desk. She looked up from her book.

"Chad, what's wrong?"

"Aubrey won't be comin' to school no more."

"Why? What happened?"

Everyone in the classroom looked at Chad.

"Because..." Chad choked. "Because her little brother, Jesse, is dead. Mrs. Foster and Aubrey are movin' back to Missouri."

Miss Bryant placed her hand on Chad's shoulder. "I'm so sorry, Chad. Is there anything that I can do?"

"No." Chad wiped a tear from his eye. "Can I go home?"

"Of course."

Chad wandered down to the creek on his way home. He sat on a rock and ran his fingers through the icy water. Chad felt empty. Life changed so quickly on the prairie.

He told his mother and father everything about the Foster family that evening. His folks decided to ride over in the morning and pay their respects to Mrs. Foster.

Chad carefully held a surprise for Aubrey in his jacket pocket, as he boarded the wagon the next morning. The smell of crispy fried chicken and homemade rhubarb pie steamed from the cloth-covered basket his mother carried.

His parents didn't say much on the way over to the Foster place.

Aubrey greeted Chad and his family when they arrived. Mrs. Foster stepped out of the doorway. She wore a black shawl around her slumped shoulders, but no veil.

"Now you know," Mrs. Foster said touching her scar. "It's not a secret anymore."

Chad's mother stepped down from the wagon. She walked up to Mrs. Foster with open arms. At first the widow hesitated, but then the two prairie women embraced and cried.

"We brought you something," Chad's mother said. She handed the widow the basket. "We're so sorry...about everything."

"Aubrey," Chad said. "This is for you." He pulled a sleepy yellow kitten from his pocket.

"It's a little young," Chad said. "But—"

"Oh, Chad. Thank you."

It was good to see Aubrey smile again, Chad thought to himself.

The rumbling of wagon wheels turned Chad's attention to the trail. Junior and his family approached the cabin in their wagon.

Junior climbed out of the wagon first, carrying a wooden cage. He stared at Mrs. Foster's face, then turned to Aubrey.

"I brought you these. They're some of my best chickens." He kicked at the dirt with the toe of his boot. "I know they won't take the place of your peacock, but I never meant no harm to your bird." Junior looked into Aubrey's eyes. "I'm sorry about your brother."

Aubrey accepted the cage of chickens. "Thanks, Junior."

Junior's mother brought warm bread and honey along with her sympathies.

"Do you have to go?" Chad asked Mrs. Foster.

The widow sighed.

"Don't go," Chad's mother said. "We'd like you to stay. Give us another chance to be good neighbors."

The widow looked at the people gathered around her, nodding in agreement.

"You want me to stay? But—"

"Please, Mama," Aubrey pleaded. "Chad's my best friend and I don't want to leave Miss Bryant."

Mrs. Foster brushed the hair away from Aubrey's face. A meadowlark sang out from a fence post.

"I didn't think anyone cared," she said to Chad. "I've been so afraid."

"I know," Chad said looking out over the prairie. "I know."

Chapter 13

Something to Celebrate

The sun shone brightly over the town of Buffalo as the statehood celebration began. Chad couldn't believe July 10th had finally arrived.

"Mama, you sure look pretty," Chad said as his mother gingerly stepped down from the wagon. In his mind he was thinking she also looked a little more plump.

"Why thank you, Chad."

"She's the prettiest gal here," his father added taking her hand.

"I bet you say that to all the gals," his mother teased.

"It's goin' to be a hot one today," his father said wiping his brow. "July can be unmercifully hot."

"Look, Mama. There's Mrs. Foster and Aubrey," Chad said waving as the two friends approached.

"Mornin', Mrs. Foster," his father said.

"Mornin'," she replied. "What a pretty dress you're wearin'," she said to Chad's mother.

"Thank you, Rose. I didn't think I would finish it for the celebration."

"Aubrey, I like the ribbon in your hair," Chad's mother said. "What do you think of Chad's new hat?"

"I think it makes him look grown up," Aubrey said with a twinkle in her eye.

Chad blushed like a prairie rose.

"You will join us for lunch, won't you, Rose? There's plenty."

"Please, Mama," Aubrey said cocking her head to the side like a little girl.

"I'd like that. I'm much obliged," Aubrey's mother said.

After the blanket had been laid under the shade of an immense old cottonwood tree, everyone sat down on it. Chad's mother set all the fixings for a great meal. There was fried chicken, biscuits, chokecherry jelly, cornbread and molasses, pickles, and fresh rhubarb pie. He could hardly wait to eat.

"Chad, everybody, I have a surprise," Chad's mother said. "We have something to celebrate besides the statehood of Wyoming." She took a deep breath. "I'm goin' to have a baby."

Chad's eyes opened wide. "A baby!"

"A baby," his mother repeated. "Sometime this fall."

"Oh, Mama. That's great!" Chad said. "Did you hear that, Aubrey. A baby."

Aubrey's mother clasped her hands together. "That's wonderful. I'm so happy for you."

"Me too," Aubrey said.

"Well then, let's eat!" Chad's father said. "It's the best way I know how to celebrate."

"Yep, let's eat," Chad said.

"You're just like your pa," his mother said.

Chad smiled and proudly said, "Yep, just like my pa."